Slowly Tommy looked at the very large grown-up standing in the doorway. He wore a sleek silver workout suit, which fit snugly across his wide shoulders. His hair was blond and shiny, gelled and combed back so perfectly, the rake marks were still visible. He carried a clipboard and had a pen behind one ear. Around his neck was a shiny chain, and in his mouth was a silver whistle, which he had just blown. His steely blue eyes panned across the sea of babies.

"I gots a bad feeling about this, Tommy," muttered Chuckie, eyeing the man's cross-trainers. "A really bad feeling."

Rugrats Chapter Books

Just Wanna
HAVE FUN

Based on the TV series *Rugrats*® created by Arlene Klasky, Gabor Csupo,
and Paul Germain as seen on Nickelodeon®

SIMON SPOTLIGHT
An imprint of Simon & Schuster Children's Publishing Division
1230 Avenue of the Americas, New York, New York 10020

Copyright © 2000 Viacom International Inc.
All rights reserved. NICKELODEON, *Rugrats,* and all related titles, logos, and
characters are trademarks of Viacom International Inc.

All rights reserved including the right of reproduction in whole or in part in any form.

SIMON SPOTLIGHT and colophon are registered trademarks of Simon & Schuster.

Manufactured in the United States of America

First Edition

4 6 8 10 9 7 5 3

ISBN 0-689-83131-5

Library of Congress Catalog Card Number 99-73850

Just Wanna HAVE FUN

by Sarah Willson
illustrated by Gary Fields

Simon Spotlight/Nickelodeon

New York   London   Toronto   Sydney   Singapore

Chapter 1

Stu Pickles sighed contentedly and took a sip of his frothy pink drink. He plucked out the little green umbrella from his glass and twirled it between his fingers.

"This sure is a great place, Deed," he said, gazing around the pool area of the Sliver of Sand Resort. Two feeble palm trees swayed on the concrete deck.

"It's just like the brochure promised—

a relaxing family vacation, all-day buffets, pool and spa, and best of all, coordinated events for the kids to do all day long while we relax. And two whole weeks of it! Who cares if the place isn't *right* on the beach? We can definitely glimpse it from here if we stand on the table."

"I think it's terrific too, Stu," Didi replied. She was lying on a lounge chair, reading a thick book entitled *Your Child, Your Fault.*

"The Relaxation and Stress-Relief Techniques classes are wonderful!" Didi continued. "The instructor is world-famous!" Then she frowned thought-fully. "Do you think Tommy and Dil are enjoying it as much as we are?"

"Oh, sure, honey," Stu replied. "They've got that nice events coordinator, Cindy, organizing all their activities, and

that impressive-looking Swedish guy, Carlssen, running the Babycize program. They're having a blast!"

"Well, the staff do seem enthusiastic," said Didi, turning another page. "I just love the costumes the waiters wear at the kids' mealtimes; I'm sure the kids love them too."

Chuckie's dad, Chas, came striding up from the beach. He wore a sun visor and carried a half-pound dumbbell in each hand. "Hi, guys!" he panted.

"My, you weren't gone very long," said Didi.

"Well, this stretch of beach is kind of short," Chas said. "The beach ends after about ten feet, and then becomes slippery boulders. But this place is still great! Look at this pool area with pool-side service and everything!"

A waiter dressed as Tarzan staggered

over with a huge bowl of tropical fruit, which he placed on a nearby table.

Chas set down his weights and strolled over to pick up an enormous coconut. He studied it for a moment, then set it down and reached for a pineapple.

"Ow!" he said as he pricked his finger on the fruit. Chas sucked on his finger before asking, "Uh, anyone for a game of Nerf Ping-Pong in the game room?"

Didi glanced at her watch. Suddenly she clapped shut her book and jumped up. "I have to find Betty! It's almost time for our Relaxation and Stress-Relief Techniques class. I wonder where she is? The instructor gets *so* upset when anyone walks in late."

Just then Phil and Lil's mother, Betty, trotted out from the spa area.

"Sorry, Deed," she said. "Howard just

had a pH-balanced, rain-forest mud treatment, and he let it dry too long. Had to crack him open with a croquet mallet!"

"Oh, dear, I hope he's all right," Didi said. "We just have time to peek in on the kids on our way. Do you think they're enjoying this vacation as much as we are?"

"Why wouldn't they?" asked Betty.

Chapter 2

"I don't like this bacation one bit, Tommy," whispered Chuckie. They were sitting on an exercise mat, along with their friends Phil and Lil, and Tommy's baby brother, Dil. About ten other babies sat with them. "This morning the Big Bad Wolf gave me oatmeal! I got so scareded, I couldn't eat it!"

"Don't worry, Chuckie," replied Tommy. "We're just here to have fun.

And that growed-up, Cindy, is nice."

They both looked over at the perky and suntanned events coordinator, who was squeaking excitedly on a cell phone while pulling a long pink strand of gum from her mouth and twisting it around her finger.

"Yeah," agreed Phil. "She lets us do anything we want. She didn't even yell when Lil ate some green finger paint."

"Or when Phil drew a picture on the wall with a marker," chimed in Lil.

PHTWEEEEEEEEEEEEET!

All the babies in the room jumped at the shrill sound of a whistle. Even Tommy's baby brother, Dil, stopped shaking his rattle and looked up from his baby bouncy seat.

The door to the exercise room suddenly opened. A long shadow fell over the babies. Slowly Tommy looked at the very large grown-up standing in the doorway. He wore a sleek silver workout suit, which fit snugly across his wide shoulders. His hair was blond and shiny, gelled and combed back so perfectly, the rake marks were still visible. He carried a clipboard and had a pen behind one ear. Around his neck was a shiny chain, and in his mouth was a silver whistle, which he had just blown. His steely blue eyes panned across the sea of babies.

The babies stopped fidgeting and looked expectantly at him.

"I gots a bad feeling about this, Tommy," muttered Chuckie, eyeing the man's cross-trainers. "A really bad feeling."

Cindy hurriedly clicked off her phone and spoke to them.

"Kids, this *very* nice man is Mr. Carlssen, the head of the Babycize program. He'll be working with *all* of you for the next two weeks."

Cindy examined her pearly pink nails as she spoke. "We are *so* lucky to *have* him!" She gestured wanly toward Mr. Carlssen, then patted her perfect ponytail.

The babies stared up at him. The room was silent, except for the sound of Dil sucking on his Binky.

Mr. Carlssen bared his front teeth at Cindy, as though it were a great effort to smile. Then he began pacing slowly back and forth in front of the babies, his hands clasped across the clipboard on his broad chest.

"I am indeed Mr. Carlssen," he began. "I yust love to work with cheeldren. I have trained many, many babies to grow up to become excellent athletes. There is *no* reason at all . . ." he said,

"that I cannot train you, too."

He looked around. His gaze rested on Chuckie's black socks before he added, "Your parents want to take home winners—*and only winners*. It is my yob to make sure that they do! So."

Just then Dil picked up a sippy cup and lobbed it at the far wall. Its top flew off, and red juice spilled everywhere. The babies gasped.

Mr. Carlssen frowned at the mess, then he shrugged as he continued. "Next week you will all compete in the Sliver of Sand Resort's Baby Olympics!"

"Baby Limpings?" whispered Chuckie. "Why are we gonna be limping, Tommy?"

"Why does that guy talk funny?" asked Lil.

"How come he's wearing big baby shoes?" Phil wanted to know.

PHTWEEEEEEEEEEEEET!

Everyone was silent again. Mr Carlssen stared at them for what seemed like a long time.

"We will start with weight lifting," he finally said, "then move on to cardiowascular." He nodded to Cindy, who started passing out tiny pink plastic dumbbells.

"Remember," said Mr. Carlssen. "I am here to teach you that *winning* is *everything.*"

Chapter 3

"Hi," panted a big baby. "I'm Baby Bobby Bubbles, but you can just call me Bubba."

"Hi," Tommy panted back. "I'm Tommy, and that's my friend Chuckie." Tommy was working on aerobic conditioning for the Wee Li'l Walker event. He was jumping up and down on a minitrampoline.

Chuckie and Bubba were next to him, sitting side by side in a toy rowboat,

pulling and pushing heavy wooden oars. Every few minutes Mr. Carlssen came by, stood in front of them with a huge bullhorn, and bellowed, "STROKE!"

"What're you here for?" asked Bubba.

"'Laxing Family Bacation," Tommy replied. "What about you?"

"'Laxing Monthlong Getaway. Me and my friend Victor over there have been here for days and days already. Our moms and dads were here on their humming-moon, and they wanted to come back with us kids."

"You guys look like you've been doing this for a long time," said Chuckie. He looked over at Victor, a large-sized baby who was running repeatedly toward a huge, padded blocking sled, driving his shoulder into it and whooping loudly.

"Yep. I'm undy-beated in the Wee Li'l Walker and the Tot Trot. Victor is the return champing in the Crib Climb."

"The Crib Climb?" repeated Chuckie.

"Mmm-hmm. Victor also plays violin, and he's a champing chess player too. And see the twins over there?" Bubba pointed toward a boy and a girl about the same age as Phil and Lil. "They are Edie and Petey—basketball players. You should see Edie's baby hook shot. Sweeeeet."

Chuckie stopped pulling. He glanced over at Edie and Petey, who were playing basketball at a baby-sized plastic hoop with Phil and Lil.

"But this is just for fun, right?" Chuckie asked worriedly. "We're here to play while the growed-ups exercise and eat a lot and stuff, right?"

Before Tommy or Bubba could reply, Mr. Carlssen noticed that Chuckie had stopped rowing. He trotted up to

Chuckie with the bullhorn.

"STROKE!"

Chuckie gulped and resumed rowing. Mr. Carlssen continued patrolling around the other exercising babies.

"Play? No way," muttered Bubba, pulling hard on his oar. "You heard what Mr. Carlssen said. If we don't win the Limpings, our parents won't want to take us home."

"They'd leave us here . . . forever?" asked Chuckie.

"Think so," Bubba replied.

Meanwhile Stu, Didi, Betty, Howard, and Chas were passing the baby exercise room on their way to the luncheon buffet. They peeked in.

"Awwwww," said Stu. "Aren't they cute, playing like they're doing real grown-up exercise?"

Didi smiled. "Look, even Dil is trying!"

She pointed at Dil, who was trying to pull himself up on a little play gym rigged with a special pull-up bar. Next to him a baby boy and a baby girl were pulling themselves up easily.

"Hey, check out our pups playing like they're shooting hoops!" bellowed Betty as she nudged Howard. She pointed at Phil and Lil. "And they're playing with another set of twins! How 'bout that!"

"Ooof!" Howard winced. "Do you think the instructors should be allowing those two kids to back into the basket like that?" He watched them a bit more, then cried out, "Look! That boy just stepped on Phil's toes! And that girl just threw an elbow into Lil!" He was just about to turn away when he spotted another move. "Those other twins just executed a perfect give-and-go," he added glumly.

"Aw, pshaw. It'll toughen up our tykes," said Betty.

Soon an athletic-looking couple wearing matching warm-up suits jogged up to them. "We're Donald and Donna Donovan," the man said to Stu, Didi, Betty, Howard, and Chas as he continued to jog in place. They peeked into the exercise room.

"Those are our twins—Edie and Petey," Donald said, beaming. "Donna started doing dribbling drills when she was four months pregnant so the babies would get used to the sound of the ball. I was showing 'em motion-offense videos before they could even sit up!"

Donna blushed. "Come on, honey," she said. "We have just enough time for three sets of lower-ab crunches before lunch. And I heard they're serving your favorite today: Sliver of Sand's Sliver of

27

Liver Sandwiches!" They jogged away.

Betty frowned and called out to Phil and Lil, "Philip! Follow through on your shot! Lillian! Get those hands in the passing lane!"

"Let's go. We probably shouldn't be interrupting," said Didi. "They look like they're having so much fun!"

She ushered the rest of the parents toward the dining room.

Chapter 4

Stu, Didi, Chas, Betty, and Howard took their seats at a large table with a few other grown-ups.

Stu picked up the flyer by his plate. "The Baby Olympics?" he read. "Looks like that Carlssen fellow is going to run it. He's planning a whole bunch of little kiddie events!"

"Oh, isn't that sweet!" said Didi. Then she wondered out loud, "Do you think we should really encourage them to participate in competitive sports like this at such a young age? It could damage their inner psyches and upset the equilibrium in their sense of self."

"Aw, Deed, it's just for fun," said Stu. "Look at this: They're even having events for the littlest ones." He chuckled. "Dil is competing in the Rattle Chuck against two other babies his age—Brittanica and Gordon."

"Brittanica is my little girl!" called a statuesque woman from down the table. "She has a wonderful arm!"

A large man two chairs down the table leaned over and clapped Stu on the back. Stu started coughing. "Name's Bubbles!" the man said loudly. "My boy Bubba is in the baby group too! You should see him on the trampoline! Kid's got a vertical leap, he does!"

Stu smiled tightly back at him. "Yeah? My boy Tommy is slated for the Wee Li'l Walker event. He's got some speed . . . I think."

"No kidding?" Bubbles hollered back. "My Bubba's in that event too. He's the returning champ. They have to build a big tower of blocks, then run at each other's tower with a baby walker to knock it down. He's also running the Tot Trot."

Chas cleared his throat. "I understand that my Chuckie is participating in that event," he volunteered.

Bubbles looked Chas up and down with some amusement. "Kid inherit his athletic ability from his dad, did he?" he guffawed.

Chas frowned and sat up straighter in his chair.

A woman across the table smiled

gaily at them. "My boy Victor just *loves* these organized events!" she said. "We've encouraged his talents in violin and chess. Who knew he was such a little athlete as well!"

Then she pointed toward Stu. "I think Victor's going to be competing in the Crib Climb against your little one! My husband is back in our room right now, mixing wheat germ into Victor's baby food!"

A man who was built like a minivan grinned heartily at the group. He thrust a catcher's mitt-sized hand toward Howard. "Name's Klondike. Defensive end, Notre Dame 'eighty-two."

Howard made a face as he pulled back his throbbing hand and quickly plunged it into his glass of ice water.

"My boy Walter is so far off the charts in height and weight, the doc had to

tape an extra sheet of graph paper to his chart!" Klondike laughed heartily as he helped himself to another leg of lamb.

After a respectful silence, Howard picked up the program and continued reading. "Look here! They've got an Iron Babe event!" he exclaimed. "The kids are supposed to crawl fifty feet, ride a push toy once around the track, then dash through a sprinkler!" He stopped reading and looked up. "Chuckie?" he wondered. "Nah. Phil? Nah."

"There's even a stroller race for parents to do with their kids!" said Betty.

Klondike stopped chewing for a moment. "I'm in that one wif Walfer and we're *defumately* gumma win!" he said as he slammed his hand on the table to show how sure he was.

"Right-ho," said Chas, picking up some of the flatware from the floor.

Suddenly the room was very quiet. The grown-ups all looked at one another with new eyes.

"We have work to do!" Stu told Didi.

"I haven't iced Brittanica's arm today," muttered Brittanica's mother.

Didi looked at Betty. "Should we postpone the Relaxation and Stress-Relief Techniques class?" she asked.

"You BETCHA!" replied Betty.

Everyone at the table pushed back their chairs and hurried off.

Chapter 5

The next day the babies were having lunch in the kids' dining room. The waiters and waitresses were again dressed in costumes.

"More cottage cheese, honey?" Little Miss Muffet asked Tommy. He put down his spoon and clamped his mouth shut.

"How about some more shepherd's pie?" Little Bo-peep said to Walter.

He gave a delighted squeal, and Bo-peep spooned another helping into his bowl.

Dil was in his high chair. He flung his rattle with all his might. It sailed through the air, making a perfect arc. It flew through the doorway, right into the dining room next door, where all the parents were being served a flaming platter of bright orange food. The rattle whizzed by Stu's ear.

"Huh?" said Stu. He looked at the rattle on the floor, then craned his neck to call out to Dil. "Atta boy, Dil!"

"Mommy is so proud of you, Dilly!" cooed Didi as she waved to him. "He threw his rattle the farthest today!" She beamed at the other parents.

Brittanica's mother cleared her throat. "Actually, my little girl's throw would have been the farthest had it not deflected off the head of the events coordinator, who was in her way."

Didi smiled coolly at her, then turned and waved at Dil again.

Meanwhile, back in the babies' dining room, the Big Bad Wolf approached Chuckie carrying a tray of crackers. Quick as lightning, Chuckie was out of his booster seat, streaking through the grown-ups' dining room, and headed outside.

Stu and Chas stared at Chuckie, astonished. Stu had been working out complicated mathematical equations on his cocktail napkin. He turned to Chas, eyebrows raised.

"Kid's got wheels," said Stu.

"Mmm-hmm," agreed Chas.

Stu opened up a small notebook and scanned a page. "Aunt Miriam's got him at sixteen to one in the Tot Trot. He's our dark horse. Smart money's on Chuckie."

"To think—*my* Chuckie!" said Chas proudly.

Stu leaned toward Chas. "Chas, you and Chuckie should represent us in the Stroller Run," he whispered.

Chas began coughing on his pu-pu platter. "B-B-But why me?" he asked, after he had recovered.

"Chuckie must have gotten his speed from his parents," said Stu, "so there's a fifty-fifty chance it came from you!" He motioned to a passing waiter, who was dressed as a gorilla. "Uh, cancel his butterscotch sundae. He'll have a wheat-grass milk shake instead," said Stu.

Chas made a face, but Stu simply added, "We'll have you take a nice, easy, five-mile warm-up run after lunch. Then we'll hit the weight room."

Chapter 6

"YUST DO IT!" Mr. Carlssen boomed at the babies. The babies were pushing baby walkers in all directions.

"Tomorrow the Olympics begin!" Mr. Carlssen called out. "I've cancelled all other activities! Your parents will be there to watch you. They will want you to succeed at *all* costs, to *win* at *any* price!"

"Your moms and dads will be so

proud!" Cindy chimed in as she checked herself out in the mirror.

"Proud?" echoed Phil to the babies. "They'll only be proud if we win our games. If we lose, our parents won't want to take us home with them."

Tommy looked at his little brother, who was chewing on a tiny dumbbell. "I sure hope Dil can win that Rattle Chuck event," he said grimly.

"Well, if Brittanica wins, you can take home a little sister instead!" said Lil brightly. "Your parents only want to take home a winner, so maybe she'll be the one!"

Tommy shook his head. "No, my mommy and daddy like Dil bestest," he said.

"But what will happen if I lose in the Wee Li'l Walker event? Maybe they'll take Bubba home instead of me.

I heard Mr. Snarlssen say Bubba was going to be a great yumper."

"What's a yumper, Tommy?" asked Chuckie, who had just joined them after trying to tumble on the mats nearby.

"I dunno," said Tommy, "but it probably looks like Bubba."

"Let's go work on our yump shots, Lillian," said Phil. "Edie and Petey have been playing with the basketball set all morning."

"Okay, Philip," said Lil.

Meanwhile, back in the swimming pool area, the parents were gearing up for the next day too.

Stu had just hung up with Aunt Miriam. "She wants a fiver on Bubba in the Wee Li'l Walker event," he said to Didi.

"She's betting against her own great-nephew?" cried Didi.

"Well, she wants Tommy for the Crib Climb, even though Victor's got five-to-one odds," Stu explained.

Chas was jogging on the treadmill while pushing a simulated stroller.

Betty was timing him with a stopwatch.

Howard was pouring sports drinks into the babies' training cups.

Victor's mother walked in. "It's time for his power nap," she told the other parents.

"We made a motivational tape for him to listen to while he sleeps. It encourages him to relax on the straightaways and lean into the curves." She hurried out.

Klondike lumbered past as he pushed Walter in the stroller. Walter was sitting on top of three huge concrete blocks.

"See ya at the starting line, Spinster!"

Klondike puffed at Chas.

Bubbles strode in and said, "I almost forgot to order Bubba's special training meal—minced steak and mashed potatoes!" He dashed off toward the kitchen.

Chapter 7

The big day finally arrived. Mr. Carlssen had a crazed look in his eyes. His usually perfect hair was mussed up. He strode around, muttering to himself. A few parents paced nervously back and forth. Some laced up booties, others gave their babies rubdowns.

Stu walked over and put his arm around Tommy. "Son," he said. "No matter what happens today, remember these words of advice."

He scratched his head. "Right. Uhh. Remember: Winning isn't everything, but it wouldn't hurt. Make your mom and dad proud! Make your little brother look up to you! Win one for the li'l sipper!" He smiled and patted Tommy's head.

PHTWEEEEEEEEET!

Mr. Carlssen blew the whistle. "Line up for the Stroller Run!" he boomed.

Stu, Didi, Betty, and Howard hurried over to the starting line to encourage Chas. Chuckie sat in the stroller, snugly strapped in and wearing a sturdy helmet.

Alongside them were three other pairs of contestants, including Mr. Klondike and Walter. Mr. Carlssen raised the starting gun. "On your mark . . . Yet set . . ."

BANG!

The strollers and parents were off—except for Chas and Chuckie.

"What's wrong, Chas?" yelled Stu.

"Stroller . . . won't . . . go . . ." panted Chas, straining to push Chuckie's stroller. They watched Walter and Klondike streak across the finish line.

The winners ran a victory lap around the pool area. Cindy handed them a huge pineapple tied with a bright blue ribbon.

Klondike acted like he had just scored a touchdown and threw the pineapple on the ground. The fruit burst into several hundred pieces.

Stu looked down at the back wheel of Chuckie's stroller.

"Something's wedged in here," he muttered. He plucked a small object out of the axle and held it up.

"A Binky?" said Didi.

"A Binky," replied Stu darkly.

"Sabotage," gasped Howard.

"Surely somebody must have dropped it in there by accident," said Chas, mopping his brow.

"Maybe," replied Stu. "But, then again, maybe *not*! This," he muttered, "means war."

"Next event is the Rattle Chuck!" called Mr. Carlssen. Everyone hurried over to where Dil, Gordon, and Brittanica sat in their baby seats.

ZIIIIIIIING!

Three rattles sailed through the air like golden arrows. Dil's flew straight and true, making a perfect arc in the sunbeams that streamed down from the high windows.

It flew toward Mr. Carlssen, who had dashed away to make arrangements for the next event, and hit the bill of his cap.

"Oh, Tommy, Dil won!" said Chuckie to his friend.

"Yeah, that's great," said Tommy with a slight catch in his voice. "Now my parents can take him home with them."

Tommy swallowed hard and looked over at the rest of his family, happily celebrating.

"Okay, listen! Now we will play BASKETBALL!" bellowed Carlssen. "This to be followed by Wee Li'l Walker, Tot Trot, Crib Climb, and then, for the grand finale, IRON BABE!"

Tommy looked over at Dil, who was in their mother's arms. Dil waved to his older brother.

Tommy looked over at Chuckie, who had taken off his glasses and was chewing on them. Phil and Lil were over at the basketball area, staring anxiously at Edie and Petey, who were helping each other stretch out.

The noise level in the room was growing louder by the minute. Tommy looked over at his father. Stu was arguing with Walter's dad, who was holding up a Binky and shouting at him. Betty and Howard were talking heatedly to Edie and Petey's parents.

Brittanica had gotten ahold of Mr. Carlssen's whistle and was blowing on it. Mr. Carlssen was waving his arms wildly, running through the room and yelling, "Win! Win! Win!" with a frenzied look in his eyes.

Suddenly Tommy felt someone clutch his shirt with clammy hands. It was Bubba.

"Tommy, this isn't any fun!" he whimpered. "I don't like that Mr. Carlssen. I don't like my mom and dad yelling all the time."

Victor walked over. "I wanna go splash in the baby pool. I don't wanna do this Limpings stuff."

At the basketball court, Phil, Lil, Edie, and Petey set down their ball and went to where the others were. "We don't wanna do any more yump shots," said Lil. "We wanna go eat some finger paint," she said.

Tommy watched Walter jump off the minitrampoline. A few cracks fanned out from where his feet hit the floor, but Walter didn't notice. He sat down and began trying to tug off the number taped to his back.

"My tummy hurts," whimpered Chuckie.

All the babies were looking at Tommy. "Well . . . guys . . ." he said slowly. He looked around at the parents. "A baby's

gotta do what a baby's gotta do. And I can only think of one thing to do right now. WAAAAAAAAAH!"

As soon as Tommy burst into tears, Bubba did too. So did Victor, Walter, Phil, Lil, Chuckie, and the rest of the babies. Soon the entire room was filled with the sound of wailing babies.

The parents stopped racing around. They ran over to their babies. "Tommy!" said Stu. "Pull yourself together, son! You have a race to run!" Then he stopped himself. He picked up Tommy and patted his back. He looked over at Didi.

"Oh, Stu, how silly we've been behaving!" said Didi.

Stu held Tommy tightly and nodded guiltily. "We sure have, hon," he said.

Bubbles came over to Stu and Didi, carrying Bubba. Klondike joined them, holding Walter. "I say we bag this Baby

Olympics!" bellowed Bubbles. Klondike nodded vigorously.

"Let's take our kids for a swim in the kiddie pool!" suggested Donna Donovan, who was holding a snuffling Petey in her arms.

"Great idea!" said Betty. Everyone left the exercise area except for Mr. Carlssen, who stared at the now-empty room in complete astonishment.

Chapter 8

It was a few days later. Stu sighed contentedly and looked over toward the kiddie pool, where Tommy, Chuckie, Phil, Lil, and several other babies were splashing around happily.

Cindy sat in the lifeguard chair, chatting on her phone as she watched the kids.

"It sure is relaxing around here since Carlssen has been moved over to dining services," Stu said to Didi.

Just then Mr. Carlssen came out to the pool area. He was dressed as Little Red Riding Hood and carried a big basket full of vegetables and dip. After glumly setting it down, he retreated quickly to the kitchen.

Suddenly Didi jumped up. "Mustn't be late! I'm due for a seaweed wrap with Betty before our stretch 'n' burn 'n' tone 'n' trim class!" she said. "Will you watch Dil, Stu? Thanks. I'll see you at supper!" And she dashed off to find Betty.

Stu looked at his watch. "Whoops, almost forgot! I've got a hot-oil heel massage. Come on, Dil." He hauled himself from the lounge chair, picked up Dil, and headed for the spa area.

In the pool Chuckie chucked a ball to Bubba, who gurgled happily and bopped it toward Victor. Victor flipped it to

Walter, whose gentle tap sent it sailing over the palm trees and onto the beach.

"Oops," grinned Walter sheepishly. The other babies giggled.

"I haven't seen the Big Bad Wolf," Chuckie said to Tommy. "Mr. Snarlssen must have scareded it away."

He grinned and added, "This bacation turned out okay after all, Tommy!"

"Yeah, Chuckie," Tommy agreed. He leaned back on his inflatable duck and sighed. "Like I always say, babies just wanna have fun."

About the Author

Sarah Willson has written more than eighty children's books, many of them about the Rugrats! She has been a newspaper cartoonist, and once played semiprofessional basketball. She lives in Connecticut with her husband, three small children, and two large cats.

Sarah is a big sports fan, and likes to write about sports in her stories whenever she can. And her children love the fact that they can have a real basketball hoop in their bedroom!